Knock out
without the punch

Written by Miss Mikayla

Illustrated by Canva

I'm sorry to have met Mr. Player,
cold rock...
Man-ipulator...
Danger...
Mr. "Uh-oh, I've been caught."

He knew how to ramble.
He knew how to bluff.
He knew how to fake it,
to look manly and tough.
He had strength and charisma,
like every girl wants,
but his motives were selfish.
What he offered wasn't love.

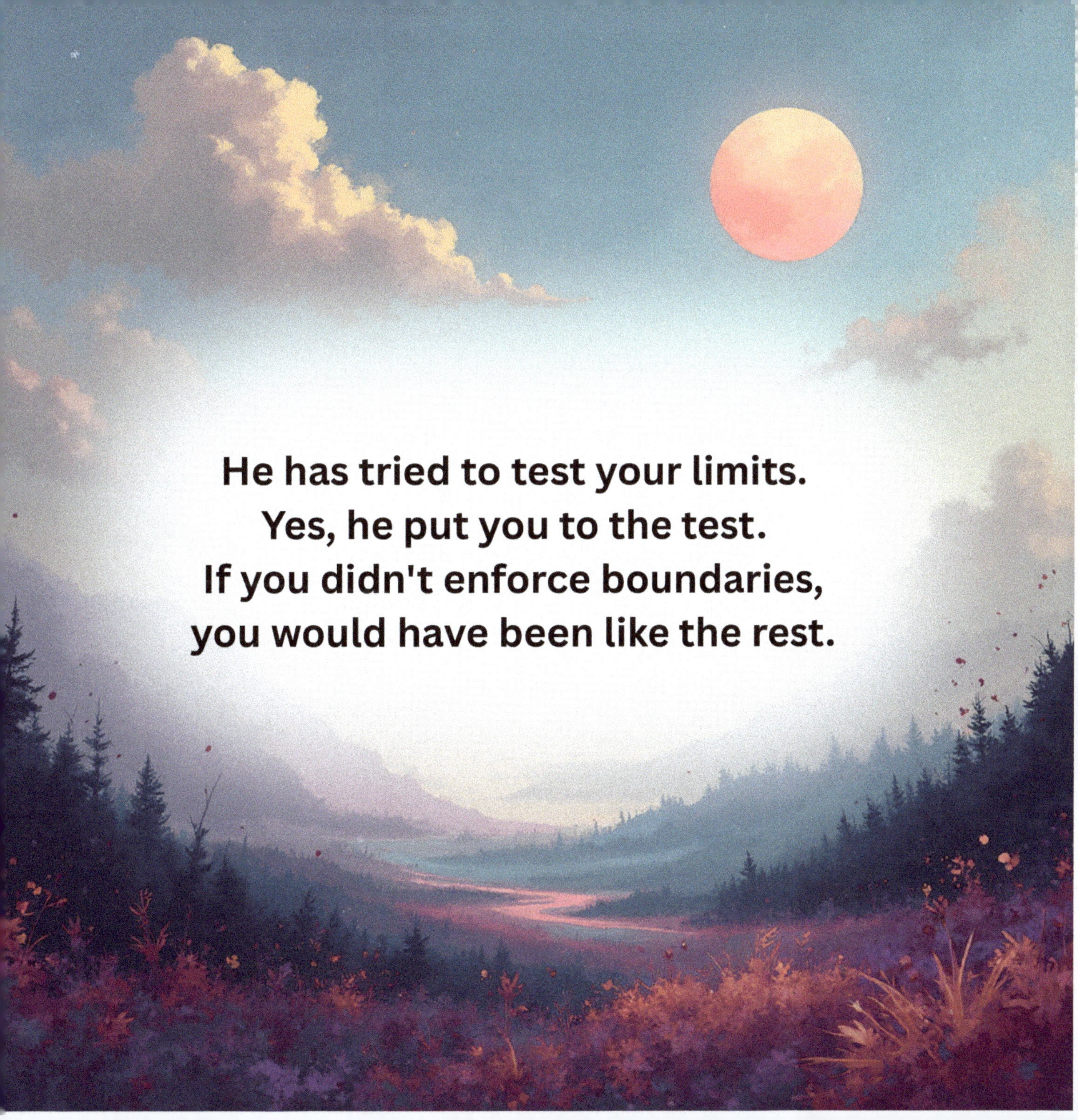
He has tried to test your limits.
Yes, he put you to the test.
If you didn't enforce boundaries,
you would have been like the rest.

He cannot tempt your spirit;
He can only tempt your flesh.
Prestige and popularity
isn't worth his worthless best.

He'll love you 'til you
challenge his free time or reputation.
He'll ponder if it's you or if the next
he should be chasin'.

He wants mammon, clout and power.
He wants social currency.
He wants control of rooms he has not entered.
He wants authority.
He wants what he's not ready for.
He wants territory.
He's been offered a place in heaven,
but he'll chase what's temporary.

Does he know how to love?
Did he have a good example?
Has he ever been heartbroken?
Is he caring? Is he humble?
If he has a heart of gold,
let God refine it in the fire.
If he has the traits I listed, then watch out.
He's in hot water.

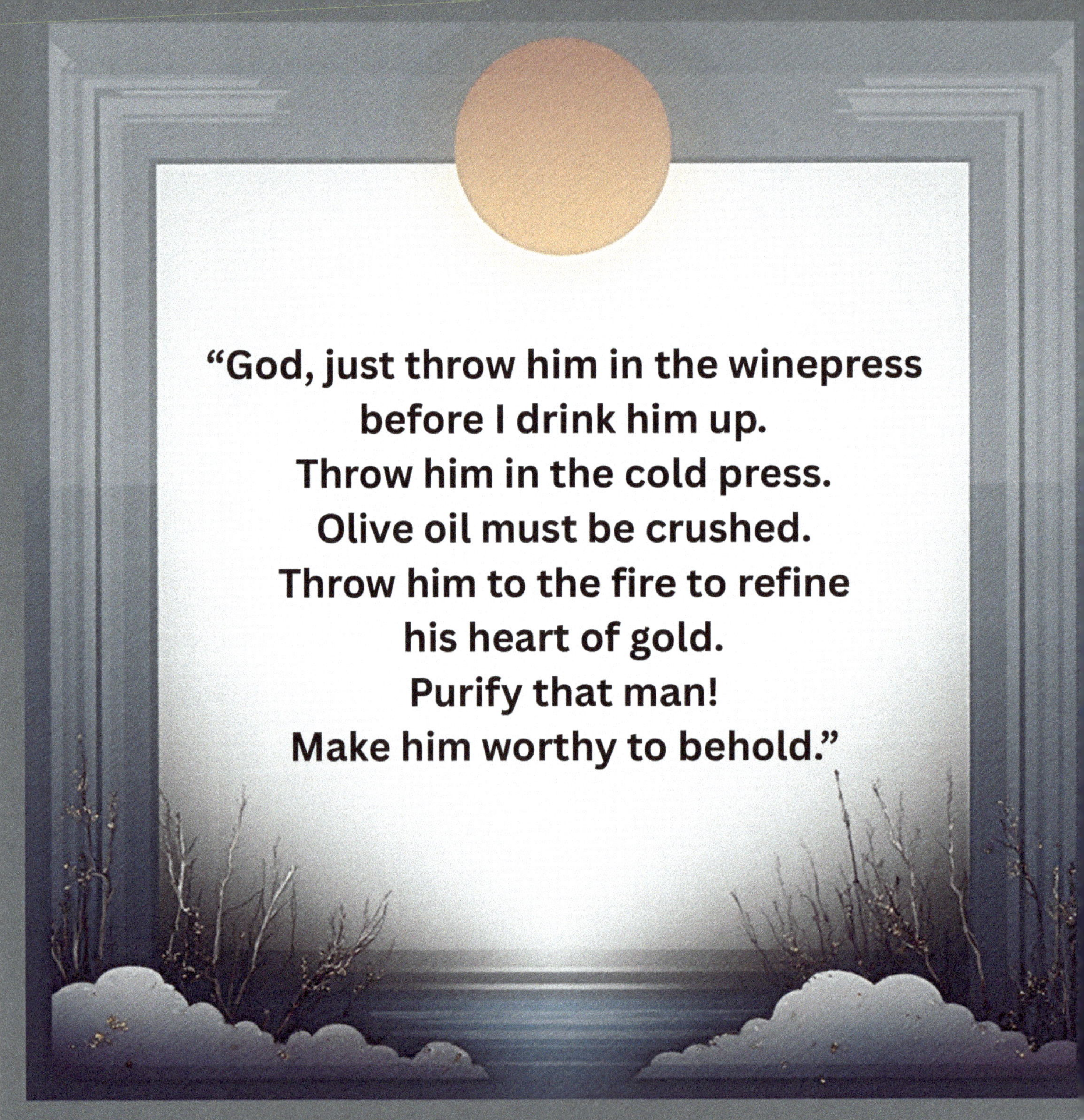

"God, just throw him in the winepress
before I drink him up.
Throw him in the cold press.
Olive oil must be crushed.
Throw him to the fire to refine
his heart of gold.
Purify that man!
Make him worthy to behold."

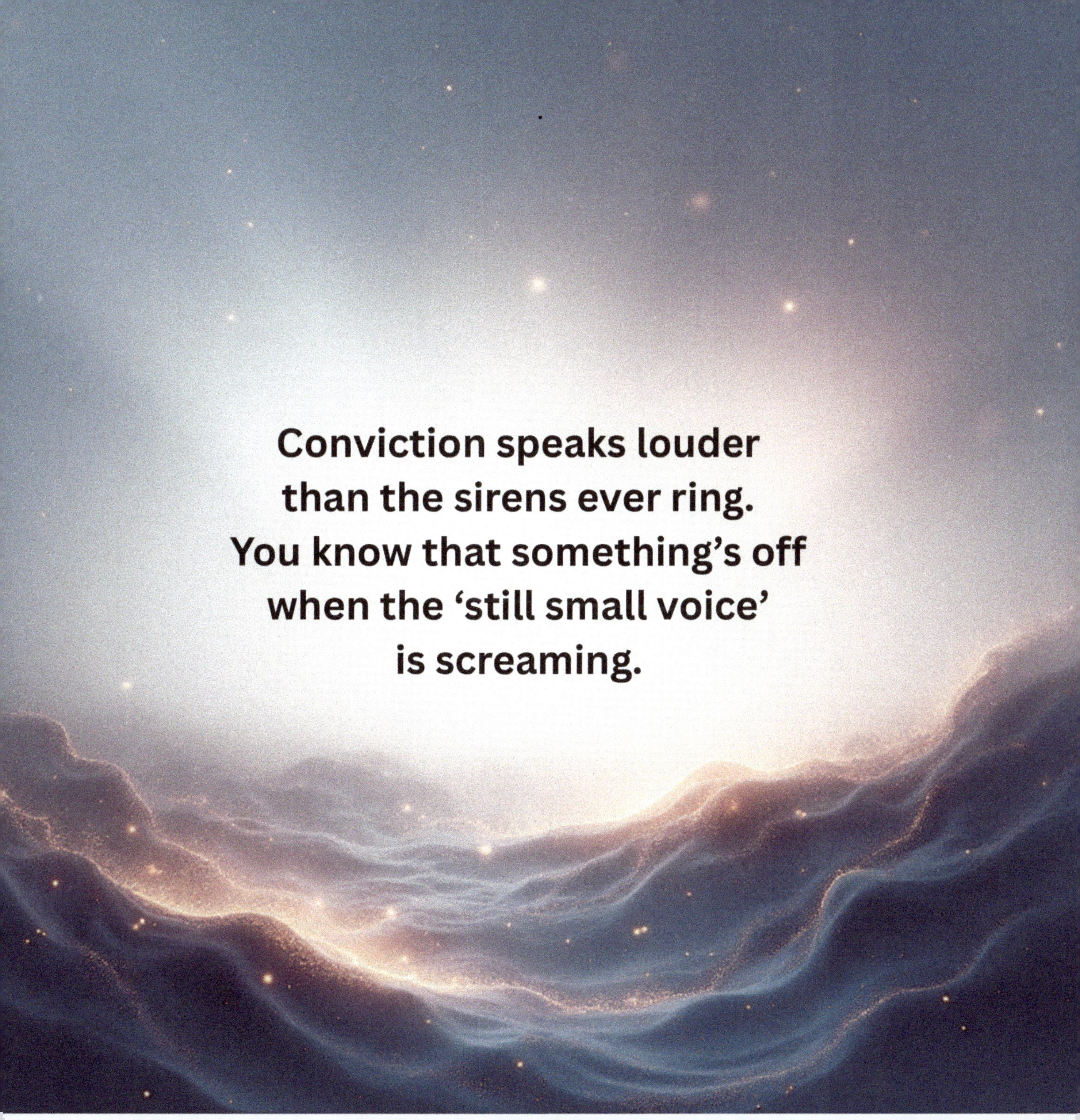
Conviction speaks louder
than the sirens ever ring.
You know that something's off
when the 'still small voice'
is screaming.

Yes, that man can ramble.
I'm glad that he can bluff,
because first responders need that skill
to rescue a loved one.
In a crime scene, he can lie, divert attention,
and assist an escape.
He's a hero in the making,
fearfully and wonderfully made.
His strength was quite convenient,
pushing a car out of the snow,
carrying your groceries, and transporting a boat.
His charisma's not for clout.
It's for speaking to the masses.
He was born to be a leader.
Let him redirect his focus.

He's a narcissist. You know it,
but he's not the one to blame.
He has value deeply buried.
God made him to do great things.
You're adding to the problem
if you're adding to his shame.
Only God can change his heart.
It's not my job to persuade.

Labeling and judging,
blocking, public shaming,
gossiping and slander,
calling out what's truly ugly,
cannot be effective in
building his Christ-identity.

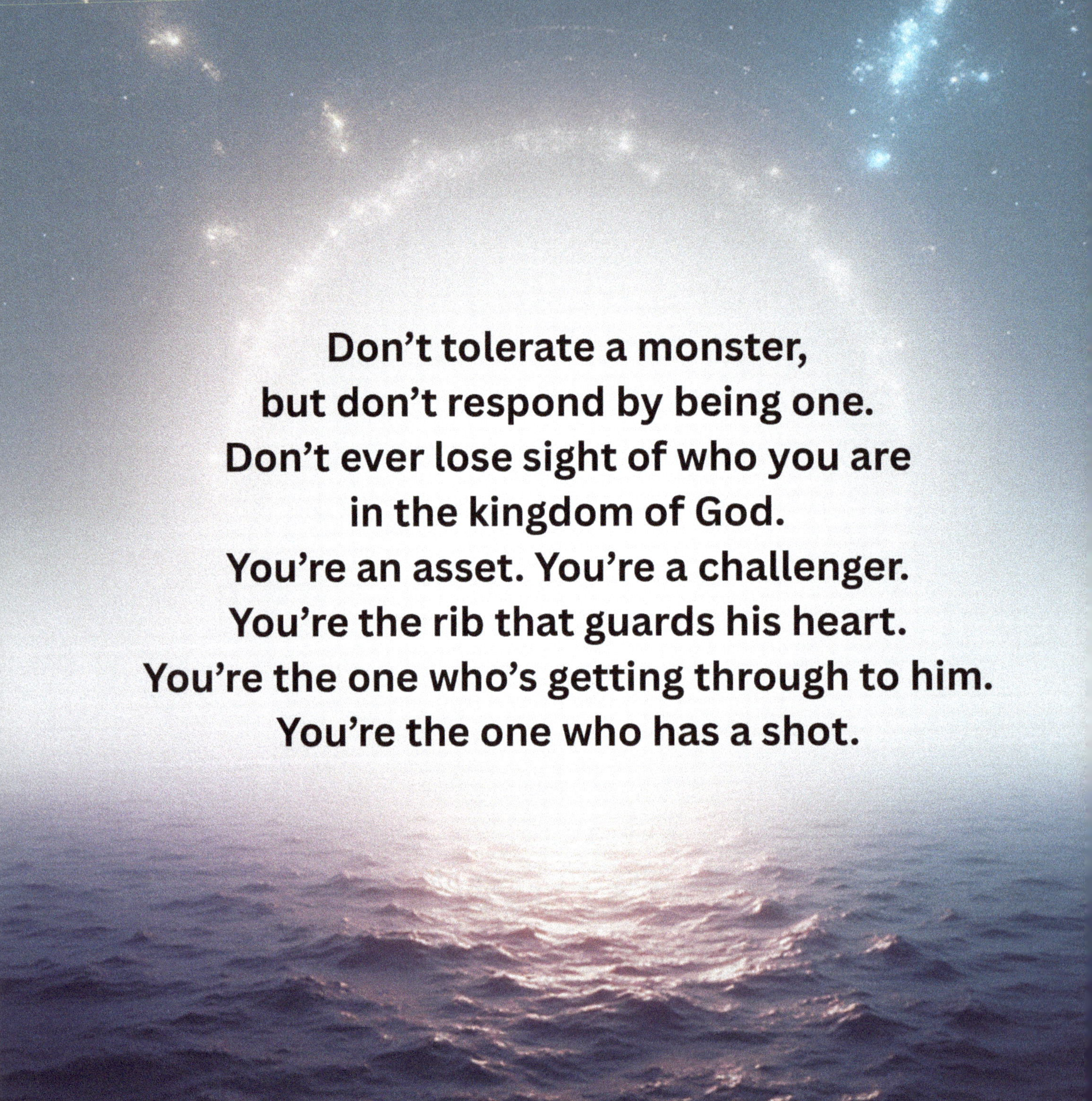

Don't tolerate a monster,
but don't respond by being one.
Don't ever lose sight of who you are
in the kingdom of God.
You're an asset. You're a challenger.
You're the rib that guards his heart.
You're the one who's getting through to him.
You're the one who has a shot.

Smear campaigns won't work with you.
The truth cannot be misconstrued.
You didn't have to take revenge.
Your sweetness exposed the truth.

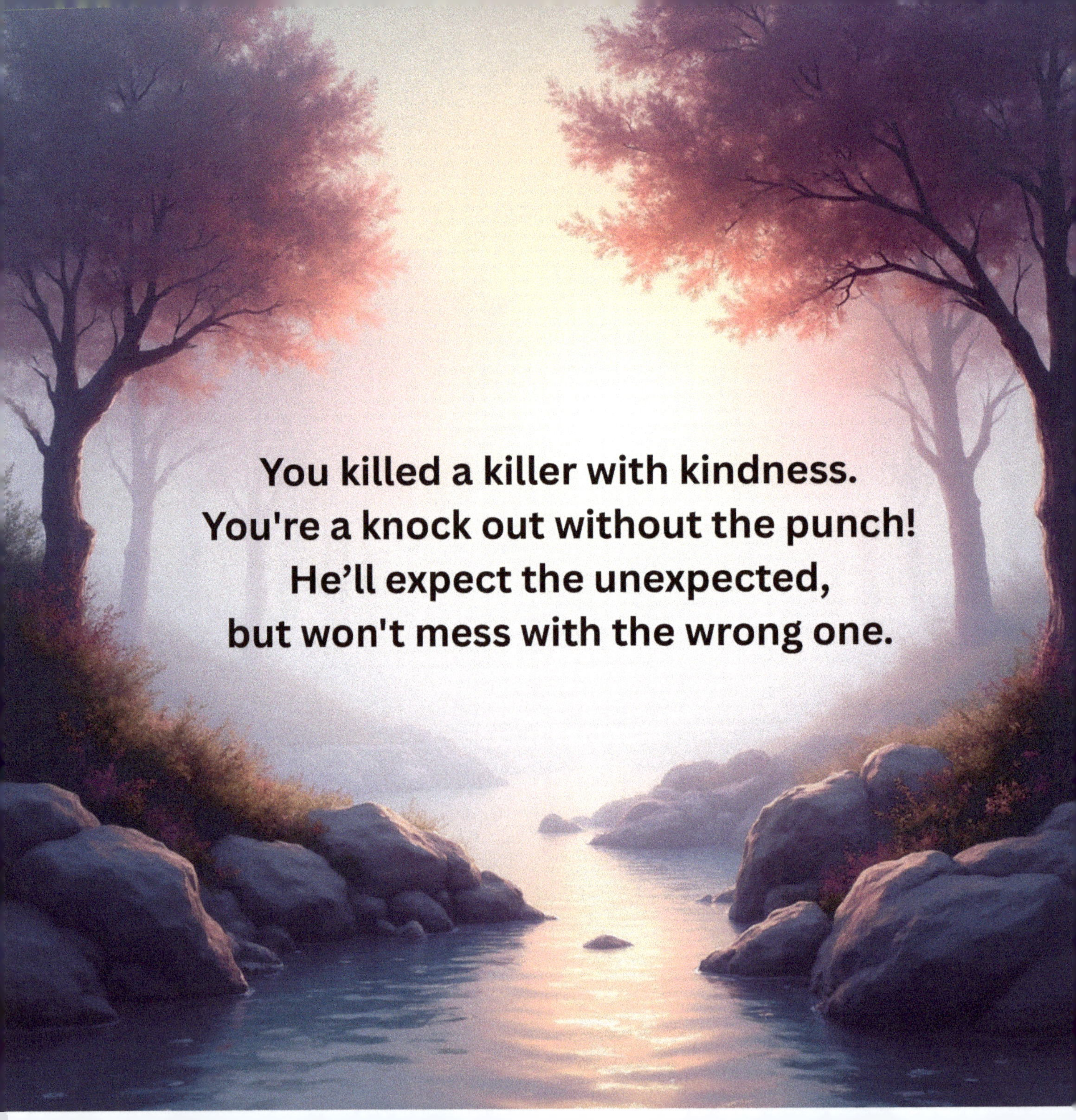

You killed a killer with kindness.
You're a knock out without the punch!
He'll expect the unexpected,
but won't mess with the wrong one.

Jimmy on Relationships
YouTube Channel

Red flags you shouldn't ignore...

For more information,
enjoy and explore Jimmy's content.
Pursue your breakthroughs!

Disclaimers:

- I'm not a psychologist. I'm a poet.

- See your mental health professional for further assistance.

- If conflict escalates to physical harm, please call the 'National Domestic Violence Hotline'. It's available 24/7 in English, Spanish, and computerized translations of 200+ languages. That number is:
+1(800) 799-7233